NINE LIVE
EMERALD, AMBER AND JET

Also in the Nine Lives Series

Ginger, Nutmeg and Clove
Daisy, Buttercup and Weed

LUCY DANIELS
Nine Lives
Emerald, Amber and Jet

Illustrated by Bill Geldart

*Hodder
Children's
Books*

a division of Hodder Headline

Special thanks to Jill Atkins

First published in Great Britain in 1999
by Hodder Children's Books

A Catalogue record for this book is available from the British Library

ISBN 0 340 73620 8

Typeset by Avon Dataset Ltd, Bidford-on-Avon, Warks

Printed and bound in Great Britain by
The Guernsey Press Co. Ltd, Guernsey, Channel Isles

Hodder Children's Books
a division of Hodder Headline
338 Euston Road
London NW1 3BH

*To Hercules, a big cuddly cat,
who was loved right to the
white tip of his tail.*

Nine Lives

Bracken is a large tortoiseshell cat who lives with the Bradman family on Liberty Street. Bracken lives a comfortable life, and spends much of her time snoozing away in her basket in the Bradmans' house.

Mr Bradman – Dad – used to be a lawyer, but he gave up this career for his real passion – gardening. He found Bracken abandoned in a skip two years ago when she was just a tiny kitten.

Mrs Bradman – Mum – is a bank manager. Unlike Mr Bradman, she loves her indoor office job.

Elsie Jennings – or Gran – is Mrs Bradman's mum. She lives a few doors away on Liberty Street. She may be over 65, but Elsie has loads of get up and go and enjoys being with children. That's why she loves her job as the local lollipop lady!

Tom Bradman is thirteen years old, and has an early morning job as a paperboy. He and his younger sister, Ellie, love animals. They always make a big fuss of Bracken and their six-year-old Golden Retriever, Lottie.

Ellie Bradman is ten years old. She's always coming up with brilliant plans and ideas – which is just as well . . . because earlier this year Bracken had her first litter. She became the proud mum of nine assorted bundles of fur . . .

Nine kittens; nine very different lives. The

Bradmans know they can't keep the kittens but they're determined that all nine go to the very best homes – homes to suit each, very special personality . . .

Emerald

1

Emerald woke with a start. *What was that?* The letterbox had rattled and something had thudded onto the doormat. *It must be Tom delivering the paper.*

She stood up and stretched, arching her back and spreading her claws.

Then she jumped down from the kitchen chair and scampered along the hallway to the front door. She was right – there was a newspaper lying on the mat.

Emerald pushed the cat flap half-open with her nose. She blinked her bright green eyes in the early morning sunlight. "Hello, Tom," she miaowed.

Thirteen-year-old Tom Bradman bent down and peered at the little shadow-grey face that appeared through the cat flap. "Hello, Emerald." Tom smiled as the rest of Emerald's small furry body followed. He knelt down and stroked her silky fur.

Emerald rubbed her head against Tom's legs. She liked Tom. She had been born in his family's house, just a few doors along from George's flat in Liberty Street. Her mum, Bracken, was the Bradmans' family cat.

Now Emerald lived with George. She had grown very fond of him, but she was glad to see Tom every day.

Tom tickled Emerald under her chin. She purred loudly to let him know she liked it.

"Well," said Tom, "I'd better get on with my paper round." He collected newspapers each day from Angie and Steve who owned the corner shop next door to George's flat.

Emerald liked Angie and Steve. They were friendly and they laughed and joked a lot. They always made a fuss of Emerald whenever she visited their shop to see her brother, Jet, who lived there with them.

Tom stood up and heaved his heavy newspaper bag onto his shoulder. "See you tomorrow," he said and he began to go down the stairs to the street.

But Emerald wasn't ready to say goodbye to Tom just yet. "I'm coming with you," she miaowed, twining herself in and out of his legs.

"Hey!" he cried, clutching the rail just in time before Emerald tripped him up. "I don't want to end up in a heap at the bottom. Go back home, Emerald."

"But I'm enjoying myself," Emerald miaowed. Now she was six months old, she was allowed outside the flat. She'd had to stay indoors when she was younger. It was much more fun being free to explore. There were so many places to hide – and things to chase and pounce on.

Emerald would go home later. She padded along the street beside Tom, wanting to play. She walked in front of him, then behind him – then in front of him again.

"Stop it, Emerald!" Tom said with a laugh. "Let me get on with my job or I'll be late for school." He took another newspaper out of his bag, folded it and pushed it through a letterbox.

Just then, Emerald heard her name being called.

"Emerald! Emerald! Where are you, you little horror?"

It was George's voice. Emerald thought about ignoring it. She didn't really want to leave Tom yet – she was having fun. But she did feel rather hungry.

Tom had heard George calling Emerald too. He bent down and gave her one last stroke. "Off you go, Emerald," he said, smiling. "George is looking for you." Then he turned round and carried on walking.

Emerald miaowed a goodbye, then she was off, streaking back along the road and up the steep steps to George's flat. She looked up at the kind old figure of George, waiting in the doorway for her.

"Here I am," she miaowed, rubbing her head against his baggy trousers.

George's grey hair hung down over his forehead as he bent forward. "I wondered where you'd got to," he said as his fingers scratched the top of Emerald's head.

Emerald followed George along the hall and into the cosy yellow kitchen, where a dishful of food was waiting for her. It smelled delicious!

"I'm going to have to keep you in if you're going to wander too far," said George, watching Emerald as she wolfed down her breakfast. "Have you been following Tom again?"

Emerald carried on eating, but she had heard his warning. She looked at him out of the corner of her eyes. *Does he mean it? Would he really keep me indoors and not let me out to explore?* she wondered.

George shook his head worriedly. "I guessed you would grow into a lively cat, but I didn't realise you would be quite so adventurous," he said.

Emerald stopped eating and looked up at George's kind, wrinkled face. "I can't help wanting to explore," she mewed. She certainly didn't want to be shut up in the flat forever. That would be terrible!

After she'd finished eating, Emerald had a

short nap, then went to find George. She found him busy shaving in the bathroom. Now she'd had a nap, Emerald felt like playing again. She leapt up onto the basin and sat in front of the big mirror. A tube of toothpaste lay nearby. Emerald decided to pounce on it. A long squiggle of white paste oozed out.

"Stop it, Emerald!" George said. He dried his face and went though to his bedroom to put on his socks and shoes.

"But I want to play," Emerald miaowed, following him. She decided to bite George's socks as he put them on.

"Stop it, Emerald!" he said again.

But when George tied his shoelaces she couldn't resist pouncing on them.

"Emerald!" George said sternly.

Emerald paused and looked up at George. He sounded annoyed. But she saw he was smiling, so she pounced on the laces again.

"Here, play with this," George said, laughing. He threw Emerald's favourite orange plastic ball across the room.

Emerald chased the ball all round the flat, pouncing on it – then hitting it to make it roll again. But she didn't like playing on her own. "Will you play with me?" she miaowed.

But George was busy reading the newspaper in the living-room now, and didn't answer her.

Emerald decided to climb the living-room curtains. She leapt at them, her claws digging deep into the flowery material. Then slowly, she climbed towards the ceiling. She loved doing this!

"Hey! Emerald!" said George, hurriedly putting down his paper. "Stop it!"

This time he wasn't smiling – he was frowning. He came over and lifted Emerald from the curtain and put her firmly on the floor.

Emerald crept under the table. She hated it when George was annoyed. She decided to go and explore outside again.

Pushing her way out through the cat flap, Emerald trotted back down the steps onto the pavement. Just then, she heard a scuffling sound behind one of the big black bins. She went to investigate.

Suddenly, a mouse shot out from behind the bins. Seeing Emerald, it froze in surprise. Emerald's eyes widened. *Oh, what fun!* she thought. Whiskers twitching, she prepared to pounce. But she wasn't quick enough. The mouse darted away. Emerald hadn't had much practice at catching mice yet. "I'll catch you next time," she miaowed.

After playing all morning, Emerald went back home to have a nap. George had settled down on the sofa to watch the afternoon film on TV. Emerald snoozed on his lap.

When the film finished, George gently lifted her off his knee and stood up. "Time I went to work," he said.

Emerald opened a lazy eye. She didn't know what "work" was, but she knew that George left her alone for a long time while he went out. She often wondered where he went to.

She followed him into the hallway where he put on his coat.

"Be good," he said as he closed the front door behind him.

Emerald looked at the closed door and then round the empty flat. She didn't feel like being inside on her own again. Suddenly she had a bright idea. *I know!* she thought. *I'll follow George and find out where he goes every day!*

She pushed her way through the cat flap and silently padded down the stairs then looked down the street to see which way George had gone. She spotted him as he disappeared round the corner into the next street.

Emerald ran after him. As she passed the corner shop, she saw that the door was open, so she peeped inside. Steve was busy serving a customer and there was no sign of Jet. Emerald turned and ran on.

By now, George was a long way ahead. He was walking very fast. The street he had turned into was much busier and noisier than

Liberty Street. Emerald dodged in and out of the legs of people rushing along.

Bang! Emerald jumped as a car door slammed nearby.

Vroom! She darted into a shop doorway as a car sped past. She could feel her heart beating very fast inside her chest.

A little girl stopped to stroke her. "What a pretty little cat," said the girl.

Emerald usually loved attention, but she had to keep up with George. "Can't stop!" she miaowed as she darted between the girl's legs and escaped. She felt the wind whistling through her whiskers as she ran faster, trying to catch up with George.

As she ran, Emerald spotted an old lady dressed in a big white coat and carrying a large round sign on a long stick. It was Tom's gran, Elsie Jennings. Emerald had seen Mrs Jennings in the big white coat before. She had sometimes worn it when she'd popped into the Bradmans' house, when Emerald lived there.

Just then, Mrs Jennings held out her big

stick – and the traffic stopped! Amazed, Emerald stopped to watch as the old lady led a crowd of children to the other side of the road.

On her way back, Mrs Jennings noticed Emerald. "Hello," she said, bending down to stroke the kitten. "It's Emerald, isn't it? I'd recognise those beautiful green eyes anywhere."

Emerald rubbed her face against Mrs Jennings' hand. "Thank you," she purred. She decided she had time to let Mrs Jennings stroke her.

"You're a long way from home," said Mrs Jennings. "You'll get trampled on here, or worse still, you'll get run over on this busy road. Let me take you home." She tried to pick Emerald up

Emerald shied away. "I'm not ready to go home yet. I'm following George," she miaowed, then turned to run on. She was just in time to spot George walk into a large building. The enormous glass doors at the entrance were surrounded by bright lights.

A long line of people were queuing up to go inside.

Why are all those people waiting to go inside? Emerald wondered. *And how come George didn't have to wait?* She was just about to follow George and find out when an enormous roaring lorry thundered towards her. Emerald's hair stood on end! She forgot all about following George. All she wanted was to be curled up safely on the sofa in George's flat.

She dashed back along the road in panic, dodging past Mrs Jennings and the little girl who had stopped to stroke her. She ran round the corner into Liberty Street, not stopping to see Angie and Steve or Jet. She leapt up the stairs and through the cat flap, then lay panting on the mat inside the door, her heart beating fast.

After a while, Emerald wandered into the kitchen and crunched a few fish-flavoured biscuits from her bowl. That made her feel much better. She decided that, despite her scare, the adventure had been worth it. I've found out where George goes every day, she thought. Next time I'll find out what he does in there.

Emerald made up her mind. She would follow George again tomorrow.

2

The next day, George left the flat much later — it was almost dark. Emerald had heard George tell a friend on the phone that he was "working the evening shift" today.

Even better, Emerald thought. Nobody would see a shadow-grey kitten in shadow-grey shadows!

She followed George as closely as she dared,

keeping to the shadows at the side of the street.

As George was passing the corner shop he pushed open the door and went in. Emerald slipped into the shop behind him.

Jet came to meet her and they greeted each other, touching noses and rubbing faces.

"Quick!" Emerald hissed to her brother. "George mustn't see me. I'm following him to find out what he does when he goes out to work for the evening."

While George was talking and laughing with Angie, Jet led Emerald to a cardboard box at the side of the shop. "If you hide behind here they won't notice you," he miaowed.

Emerald and Jet sat watching George.

After a few minutes he left the shop and Emerald slipped out behind him.

"Thanks, Jet!" she miaowed, then padded after George round the corner and onto the busy street.

But at this time of day, it was much less busy. There weren't so many people about –

and there was less traffic to be frightened of. No one stopped to stroke Emerald. And Mrs Jennings was nowhere to be seen.

The large building surrounded by lights came into view. Now it was dark outside the lights looked even brighter and more exciting. Again, George ignored the queue of people and walked straight in, through the big glass doors.

Emerald stared up at the bright lights and the enormous posters on the walls. One showed a huge ship and another showed the full moon shining down on an old house.

"Can't wait to see this film," said a man in the queue of people, waiting to go in.

"Nor can I," said the woman with him. She shivered. "It's going to be really scary."

Emerald looked up. She'd seen the couple who were talking before. They were friends of George.

"Nothing scares me," said the man, grinning.

"Lots of things scare me!" miaowed

Emerald. Just then, the glass doors were opened wide and the queue began to shuffle slowly into the building. Emerald crept past the queue and inside. There were more bright lights past the glass doors, and a woman sitting behind a counter, looking very busy. But there was no sign of George.

"Oh, no!" miaowed Emerald to herself. "What shall I do now?" She decided to hide in a corner and see if George would come back. When the couple she had heard talking outside came in, they were still talking about scary films.

Suddenly, Emerald spotted George coming through some swing doors. *How strange!* she thought. It looked as though the room he was coming from was very dark!

George saw the couple and grinned. "Hi, you two," he said, "Looking forward to being frightened out of your wits?"

"Is this film as good as they say, then?" asked the man.

"Brilliant!" said George. "One of my favourites!"

"Most films are your favourites!" laughed the woman. "That's why you work at the cinema!"

"True!" laughed George.

"Oh," Emerald miaowed quietly to herself. "A cinema?"

George turned and walked back through the swing doors into the dark room. Emerald wasted no time. She shot silently from her corner and through the doors just before they shut.

The dark room was huge! And it was warm. Emerald loved feeling warm. She loved all the warm spots at home, like in front of the fire, or snuggled up on George's knee, or in a patch of sunlight on the carpet.

Emerald didn't mind the dark either. She could still see everything that was going on. There were rows and rows of seats, all facing the same way, with people sitting in them. George was walking up and down the aisle shining a torch in front of him then flashing the torch at the seats so the people could see which ones were empty.

Emerald watched George's friends from outside go and sit near the front. Then George went out through the swing doors again.

Emerald decided to stick around to see what would happen next. She found an empty seat right at the back. It was soft and velvety, so she pushed her front paws into it, up and down, over and over again. It felt lovely! It reminded her of when she used to press her paws into her mum's tummy when she wanted some milk.

Emerald settled down and looked around her. Now she was higher up and found she was facing an enormous screen. It was like the TV in George's flat only much much bigger.

Suddenly, there was loud music, and pictures started flashing across the screen.

A ghostly-looking house, like the one on the poster outside, came into view. The moon was shining in a dark sky and grey clouds were rushing across it.

Emerald was enjoying herself. It was very warm and cosy here. Slowly, her eyes began to droop. All this excitement had worn her out! She decided to have a quick snooze . . .

Crash! Emerald woke with a start. At first she wondered where on earth she was. Then she saw the huge screen and remembered where she was. On the screen, a storm was raging. Thunder and lightning were crashing around the spooky house in the film. A man was creeping around outside the house. Emerald thought he looked a bit frightened!

She yawned and stretched, then decided to explore a bit more. She jumped down from her seat and silently stole along the aisle beside the rows of seats. She looked at the people watching the film. Lots of them were gripping the sides of their seats or holding on to the person next to them. Some had staring eyes. Some had their mouths wide open. Some were chewing their fingernails. *How strange!* she thought.

Emerald wondered if George's friends were scared too. She decided to look for them. But where were they? It would be hard to find them in such a big place. Then she remembered that they were somewhere near the front. She would creep towards the screen and try to find them.

Emerald was halfway to the front when something made her look up. She blinked. Then she blinked again. Right in the middle of the screen was an enormous, shadow-grey cat, just like her!

The cat stalked across the screen. Emerald's eyes opened wide. It was huge! "I wonder why it's in the film," she miaowed, but nobody heard her.

The music in the background started getting louder and faster. It made Emerald want to dance. So she chased her tail and jumped on pieces of popcorn that people had dropped on the floor. But no one seemed to notice her. What was going on?

Emerald looked up at the cat on the screen. She decided it would be fun to copy it. When

the cat on the screen stretched, Emerald stretched. When it crept across the screen, Emerald crept slowly towards it. She crept closer and closer.

Then the shadow-grey cat on the screen vanished.

"Where's it gone?" Emerald miaowed. Perhaps if she jumped onto a seat she'd get a better view. But there didn't seem to be any empty ones nearby. So Emerald decided to jump onto the back of a full one.

Suddenly, the people in the row behind began to gasp and scream. Emerald crouched low in fright and gripped the seat tightly with her claws.

What had happened?

She ran along the row, behind people's heads, trying to see what had scared everyone. And then she saw that everyone was looking at her!

"It's come to life!" shouted a woman. "The ghost cat in the film – it's here – in the cinema!"

Emerald was pleased with herself. *I must*

have pretended to be the cat on the screen very well! She thought. *Perhaps I'll do it some more!* She began to pretend she was the cat on the screen again, copying its movements as she walked along the back of the seats.

Now, everyone was noticing Emerald pretending to be the shadow-grey screen cat. People screamed and shouted all around her, and the noise was getting a bit frightening. Emerald didn't know what to do.

Then, above all the other shouts, Emerald heard a familiar one. "Emerald!" she heard.

It was George! Emerald miaowed back to him. "Help me, George!" Then she jumped down from the chair back and raced into the shadows towards him.

"The ghost cat's disappeared!" she heard, as George scooped her up.

"That was weird!" someone else said.

"And scary!"

Just then, the film finished, and as the main lights of the cinema clicked on, George slipped outside with Emerald and took her into a small, dark room.

"Emerald, how on earth did you get here?" George said, shaking his head. "I'm going to be in big trouble now – you've scared the audience half to death!"

Suddenly, the door burst open and a red-faced man stormed in. When he saw Emerald his eyes widened. "Who does that cat belong to?" he boomed.

"Me, Mr Skinner," said George quietly.

Mr Skinner went even redder and more angry-looking. "Right George," he shouted. "I want a word with you in my office. Now!"

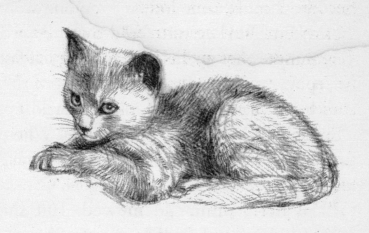

3

I don't think I like him, thought Emerald, as George followed Mr Skinner out of the room.

Emerald crept under a table, feeling very worried for George. It was her fault he was in trouble. *I wish I hadn't been so curious. I wish I'd stayed at home in the flat*, she thought.

Slowly, the noise of people talking about

the ghost cat became less, as everyone went home. Emerald began to feel drowsy. After a few minutes her eyes closed and she fell fast asleep.

A bright flashing light woke Emerald up. "Emerald," George was whispering. "Where are you? Come out. It's all right. I'll take you home."

"I'm here," Emerald mewed. But she stayed hidden in her dark corner. She was worried that angry Mr Skinner might be with him.

George's torch beam slowly came nearer. It flashed around Emerald, across her, then it stopped right on her. "So there you are, you little horror!" he said.

Emerald couldn't decide whether he sounded cross or not, but she knew she could trust him. She would be safe with him. He would take her home. "I'm so glad to see you, George," she miaowed.

A few minutes later, she was tucked inside his coat, snuggled down under his chin. She purred as George walked briskly along the main road and round the corner into Liberty Street. Everywhere was very still and quiet. Emerald guessed it must be the middle of the night. George climbed up the stairs and unlocked the door of his flat.

"I'm keeping you in for the rest of the night," he said as he put Emerald on the floor. "We don't want any more trouble."

She watched him lock the cat flap. "I don't mind – I've had enough adventures for one day!" she miaowed, twining herself round George's legs. "I'm sorry if I got you into trouble."

But George didn't stroke her or pick her up. Emerald thought he seemed upset.

Early next morning, when the newspaper thudded onto the mat, George and Emerald were already awake. They both hurried over to the door and George opened it. Tom was standing outside.

"Hello!" he said to George. "I didn't expect to see you up so early! I was waiting to say

'Good morning' to Emerald!"

Emerald purred.

"I couldn't sleep," said George. "So I thought I might as well get up early for a change."

Emerald looked up at George. He certainly did look very tired. And it was all her fault.

When Tom had gone, George went and slumped in an armchair, looking miserable. Emerald jumped up and sat on the arm of the chair beside him. She was glad when George stroked the top of her head and began to talk.

"My manager was so angry," he said sadly. "He told me I can't work at the cinema any more. He said I shouldn't have let my cat follow me to work. I told him I didn't know you were there until you suddenly leapt up and terrified everyone."

"I'm sorry!" Emerald miaowed. She rubbed her head against his hand. She hoped he could tell she was sorry.

"I loved that job," said George, "because I got to see all the latest films."

Emerald crouched low and nuzzled against his shoulder. "I hope you'll forgive me," she miaowed. "I couldn't bear it if you didn't."

George sat miserably in the flat all day. Then, as it began to grow dark, the phone rang.

George went into the hall and picked up the receiver. "Hello," he said quietly. "Oh . . . yes, sir . . ."

Emerald sat down next to him to listen.

"Oh," said George, looking surprised. "Really?" He began to sound excited. "Thank you, sir."

Who was it on the phone? What was George getting excited about?

"Oh yes, sir," said George. He beamed down at Emerald. "I'm sure she will. I'll see you as soon as I can. Goodbye."

He put the receiver down and rushed over and picked Emerald up. "Well done, you young mischief!" he said.

Emerald purred. She liked it when she made George happy, but what had she done?

"That was Mr Skinner, my manager," said

George, excitedly. "He said that there is a huge queue building up outside the cinema to see the horror film. All the people that saw you last night have told their friends. They loved you because you made the film so much more scary. And now everyone wants to see if the ghost cat will turn up again!" George chuckled. "They say seeing you was the best bit!"

Emerald snuggled against George's shoulder.

"So," George went on, "Mr Skinner wants me to take you to the cinema right now, so you can pretend to be the ghost cat again."

Emerald miaowed loudly. She had never thought of herself as a scary cat before, but the more she thought about it, the more she liked the idea!

"I'd love to," she purred. "It'll be great fun!"

"But we mustn't tell anyone," said George. He put Emerald down and pulled on his coat. "It's to be a secret. And I'll have to hide you in my coat as we go past the queue," he said, opening the door. "Come on, Emerald. We have to hurry!"

Emerald scampered behind George as he ran down the steps, along to the corner and past the shop where Jet sat in the doorway washing himself. Emerald stopped to talk to her brother.

"Where are you going, looking so pleased with yourself?" miaowed Jet.

"I'm to be the star of the show," miaowed Emerald proudly. "Only it's a secret."

"Star of the show? Secret?" miaowed Jet. "What are you talking about?"

"I'll tell you about it later," miaowed Emerald.

"Come on, Emerald," called George. "We mustn't keep your audience waiting!"

With her head and tail held high, Emerald caught up with George. Then they hurried off to the cinema.

As they drew nearer, George picked Emerald up and hid her in his coat. They went past the long queue of excited people and through the big glass doors.

The manager was just coming out of his office. He caught George by the elbow. "Have you got her?" he hissed.

George opened the top of his coat and Emerald saw Mr Skinner peering in at her.

The manager grinned, "And do you think she'll do it?"

"Let's hope so," whispered George, kissing Emerald on the top of her head.

"You'll see," Emerald mewed quietly.

Some time later, Emerald crept silently into the dark. All the seats were full and everyone was watching the film, wondering if they would see the ghost cat, like yesterday's audience. Little did they know that Emerald was about to frighten them out of their wits! And this time, she wouldn't be scared by their screams and shouts. She was going to have the time of her life!

Emerald crept like a shadow towards the front. She lay low, ready to leap out at exactly the right moment.

As the screen cat disappeared, Emerald

jumped on top of a seat back and began to make her way along the row. What a noise the people made!

As she had done the night before, Emerald jumped into the shadows when she reached the end of the row, then went to hide with George until all the people had left.

Soon afterwards, Mr Skinner burst in to George's little room again. But this time he didn't look angry – he looked very pleased. "Well done – er – Emerald!" he said with a beaming smile. "You're a star!"

Then he turned to George. "I'd like you to have your job back, George," he said. "With a pay rise – as long as Emerald comes with you!"

"Of course!" laughed George. "Emerald loved having everyone watch her. I'm sure she'd like to do it every night!"

Emerald purred and rubbed her face against George in agreement. She rather liked being star of the show. But even better – she got to come to work with George!

Amber

1

Amber scampered towards the back door. She had heard Mr Bradman's voice and that meant Lottie, the Bradman's Golden Retriever, would be home from her walk. Amber found Lottie and Mr Bradman in the kitchen.

"I'm glad you're back," Amber purred happily. Lottie bounded over to Amber and licked the kitten's nose. "We've had a great walk!" she barked.

Amber looked up at Lottie's friendly face. "I wish I could have come," she miaowed. "Where did you go?"

"Along by the river," Lottie barked.

"I can see that!" Amber miaowed, looking at Lottie's big soft-padded paws. "Your paws are all muddy."

Mr Bradman finished taking off his muddy boots, then grabbed an old towel from under the sink. "Come on, Lottie," he said. "Let's clean you up a bit."

Lottie went over to Mr Bradman, Amber trotting happily underneath her, running in and out of her legs. Amber knew that Lottie would be careful not to tread on her friend.

Tom was sitting at the kitchen table doing his homework. He laughed. "Those two are great together, aren't they?" he said. "And in a funny way they look alike because their coats are such a similar colour."

"Yes, and you'd think Amber was a puppy not a kitten, the way she behaves!" chuckled Mr Bradman.

"I wish I was!" miaowed Amber.

"Lottie's so good with all the kittens," said Tom. "But Amber's definitely her favourite."

"Of course I am," purred Amber.

"They'll miss each other when we find Amber a new home," said Mr Bradman.

"But I don't need a new home," miaowed Amber. "I'm very happy here, thank you."

Mr Bradman began to wipe Lottie's paws with the towel. Amber pounced on one corner and tugged at it with her claws.

Bracken was sitting in the cat basket in the corner, washing Amber's sister, Clove.

"Don't be a nuisance, dear," she miaowed at Amber.

"I'm not," miaowed Amber. "Lottie loves having me around. But I wish I was allowed to go for a walk with her."

"Cats don't go for walks," Bracken miaowed back.

"Why not?" asked Amber.

But Bracken was too busy cleaning behind Clove's ears to answer.

It wasn't fair! Amber thought. Why

couldn't a kitten go for a walk? "In that case, I wish I was a dog!" she miaowed.

"Don't be silly, dear," miaowed Bracken. "Anyway, you're too young to be allowed out."

When Mr Bradman had finished cleaning Lottie, she went to her water bowl to have a drink. Her long floppy tongue lapped the water noisily. Amber ran over and put her front paws on the opposite side of the bowl. Copying Lottie, she lapped away with her tiny tongue.

Tom laughed then got up from the table and reached into a cupboard. "Watch this, Dad," he said, fetching out some dog biscuits. "Here, Lottie," he called.

Lottie left her water and ran to Tom, her tail wagging furiously. Amber trotted at her heels.

"Lottie, sit," said Tom. Lottie sat down. Amber sat beside her.

"Good girl, Lottie," said Tom. "And good girl, Amber!"

"Woof!" barked Lottie.

"Woof!" miaowed Amber.

"Shake paws," said Tom. Lottie lifted a front paw and shook Tom's hand. Amber did the same.

"Good girl, Lottie," said Tom, giving her a dog biscuit. "Good girl, Amber," he said, giving her one too.

Amber loved them. They were much more tasty than cat biscuits – and much bigger!

The next morning, when Tom came home from his paper round, he found Lottie gnawing at a large bone with the tiny golden kitten beside her, as usual. Amber's teeth weren't fully grown yet, but she was copying everything that Lottie did.

Lottie stopped chewing when she saw Tom, so Amber stopped, too. And when Lottie ran to greet Tom, Amber was right behind her. Lottie barked and rolled over for Tom to tickle her tummy. Amber did the same.

"Hello, Lottie's little shadow!" Tom laughed and tickled Amber's tummy, too.

"I like that," purred Amber, rubbing the side of her cheek against Tom's hand.

Mrs Bradman came into the kitchen. She opened some tins and tipped food into several bowls. Then she banged the fork on the side of a tin and Bracken arrived with some of Amber's brothers and sisters.

They went over to the bowls of cat food, but Amber followed Lottie to wait for the dog food bowl.

"Mum," said Tom putting the last dish of food down on the kitchen floor, "I think I've found someone else who'll have a kitten."

"Good," said Mrs Bradman. "Who?"

Amber pricked up her ears and listened.

"The Green family along the road," said Tom. "It's Sam's ninth birthday next week and he's asked for a kitten. They've never had a cat before, only dogs, but they said they'd like to come round tomorrow and choose one. Is that all right?"

"Of course," said Mrs Bradman.

"They'd better not choose me," miaowed

Amber, with her mouth full, as she moved nearer to Lottie.

The next afternoon after school, Sam Green and his mother arrived at the Bradmans' house. Amber wasn't at all interested – until she noticed that they'd brought three dogs with them!

There was one who looked a little like Lottie, but with a shorter coat. And there was a white one, covered in black spots. And

the third one was short – not much taller than Amber – but long and sausage-shaped.

"We thought the dogs ought to come," said Mrs Green, as they came into the sitting-room. "There's no point getting a cat that's terrified of dogs."

"And you'll have to make sure all the dogs are willing to live with a cat!" said Mrs Bradman.

"Woof!" "Woof!" "Woof!" barked the three dogs as soon as they saw Bracken and her kittens. The cats bolted upstairs, hissing and spitting as they ran – except Amber.

She stayed beside Lottie who greeted the dogs with interest. They touched noses and walked round each other, sniffing and wagging their tails. Amber tried to do the same.

"That's amazing!" said Mrs Green.

"Wow!" said Sam. "That kitten isn't afraid at all!"

Amber looked up, surprised. "Of course I'm not," she miaowed.

"And she's so sweet!" said Mrs Green,

crouching down to get a closer look. "Have you given her a name?"

"We call her Amber," said Tom.

"Mmm, it suits her. I think we'd call her that if we chose her," said Mrs Green.

Sam nodded. "All the dogs seem to like her," he said. "And so do I!" He bent down to stroke the kitten. "Can we have her?"

"But I live here," miaowed Amber, scampering away to hide behind Lottie.

A week later, Sam arrived with his father, carrying a large cardboard box with handles on the top. Amber had almost forgotten about him choosing her. She dashed into the kitchen. Lottie was lying across the mat in front of the boiler.

"Don't tell them I'm here," Amber miaowed, and she burrowed under one of Lottie's front legs, hoping the Golden Retriever's coat would cover her.

She stayed as still as she could, but her heart was pounding so loudly she was sure everyone would notice her. She listened as

Mrs Bradman brought Sam and Mr Green into the kitchen.

Tom and Ellie ran in from the garden.

"Hello," said Tom. "Happy Birthday! Have you come for Amber?"

"Yes," said Sam, fidgeting from one foot to the other. "I've been dying to come and fetch her all week."

"She was here a moment ago," said Mrs Bradman. "I wonder where she's gone."

"I've been to the library," said Sam, as everyone searched for Amber. "And I borrowed loads of books on kittens. I know all about how to look after one now."

"That's good," said Mrs Bradman, peering under the kitchen table. "I'm glad you're going to look after her so well."

Not as well as Lottie does, thought Amber.

"And I've had some birthday money," Sam went on. "I went to the pet shop after school today and bought a special cat basket for her and a clockwork mouse and a little ball with a bell in it. Do you think she'll like them?"

"I'm sure she will," said Mrs Bradman.

No I won't! thought Amber. *I've never played with cat toys. Only dog toys!*

"Now where is that kitten?" said Mrs Bradman.

Mr Green bent down to stroke Lottie. "Hello, you're a lovely dog," he said. Then he began to smile. "What's this little thing, hidden in your fur?"

"You crafty thing!" Tom laughed as he crouched down and lifted Amber very gently from her hiding place.

"She's very sweet!" said Mr Green.

"I'm sure she'll be very happy with you," said Mrs Bradman.

"But I want to stay with Lottie," miaowed Amber.

At that moment, Bracken crept into the room and sat in a corner, well away from the dogs. Tom put Amber down next to her mum for a moment.

"Be good," said Bracken, licking Amber's nose. "You're going to be fine with three dogs to follow around!"

Before Amber could reply Tom had picked

her up again for Ellie and Mrs Bradman to say goodbye.

"Goodbye," she miaowed pitifully at each of them. Then she looked down at Lottie who was wagging her tail. "I'll really miss you," she miaowed.

"And I'll miss you, too, my little friend," Lottie woofed, "But you've got some new doggy friends at Sam's house. You won't be lonely. Good luck!"

2

The first thing Amber saw when the box opened a few minutes later was a white face with black spots peering down at her. It was one of the Greens' dogs.

"Remember me?" she miaowed.

"You're Lottie's little friend," woofed the Dalmatian. "You've come to live with us, haven't you?"

"Out of the way, Jordan," Amber heard,

as Sam reached into the box and lifted her out. After giving her a quick cuddle he put her down on the carpet.

Amber dashed up to Jordan. "So are we going to be friends then?" she miaowed nervously.

Mr Green laughed. "This one certainly likes dogs!" he said.

Jordan bent down to give Amber a curious sniff. "Lottie told us you were unusual for a cat," he woofed.

Amber rubbed the side of her face against Jordan's long, bony legs. "I like you already," she purred.

"And you're quite a sweet little thing," Jordan woofed back.

Amber followed him into the kitchen. Everything looked very different from the Bradmans'. "Where are the other dogs?" she miaowed.

"In the garden," woofed Jordan. "They'll be in soon."

If the other two are as friendly as Jordan, maybe it won't be too bad here after all!

Amber thought to herself.

Sam came into the kitchen, smiling and holding something in his hands. "Here you are, Amber," he said. "A clockwork mouse." He put the mouse on the floor in front of her.

Amber looked at it. It didn't smell like a mouse. She didn't trust it one little bit, so she began to back away.

Suddenly, the mouse made a strange whirring noise and started to skim across the kitchen floor. Amber arched her back as the mouse came towards her. "Get away from me!" she hissed and ran behind Jordan.

"Don't you like it?" asked Sam.

"Get away from me!" Amber hissed again as the mouse came nearer, but at last it slowed down and stopped.

Sam picked it up. "Oh dear," he said. "I bought it specially for you. I thought all cats liked toys like this."

"Well, I don't," miaowed Amber. "I'd rather play with Jordan."

But Sam didn't seem to understand. "I've

got some more toys," he said. "And a basket for you. Let's try that." He picked Amber up and placed her in the new basket.

Amber didn't feel as comfortable in there as she had in Lottie's basket. It didn't smell right and she didn't want to stay in it.

Just then, she heard a scratching sound on the back door. Sam went to open it and, while he wasn't looking, Amber jumped out of the uncomfortable basket.

A Labrador bounded in, "Hey, Buster!" said Sam.

Buster skidded to a stop and sniffed Amber. "Remember me?" she miaowed.

"Of course," barked Buster and he licked her nose. It reminded Amber of Lottie and made her feel much more at home.

And then the third dog galloped into the kitchen, yapping loudly. "Hi, Laddie," said Sam. "Come and say hello to the new kitten."

"Oh, you're here at last!" yapped Laddie, giving her a friendly sniff. Laddie, a small, red Dachshund, was low enough for Amber to sniff back. That made her very happy!

For the rest of the evening, Amber followed the three dogs around. She played with them, ate with them, and that night, she went to sleep curled up with Buster, the Golden Labrador. As she fell asleep under one of Buster's gentle paws, Amber realised she was having too much fun to miss Lottie.

The next morning, Amber woke when Tom pushed the Greens' newspaper through the letterbox. She heard Sam running downstairs to open the front door and scampered into the hall to see her old friend.

"Hello, Amber!" Tom said, "Have you settled in well?"

"Yes, thanks," miaowed Amber.

"She's fine," said Sam, "thanks to the dogs! But she isn't interested in the cat toys or the new basket I bought her."

Tom laughed. "We always said that Amber thinks she's a dog!" he said.

Just then, Buster bounded into the hall, took the newspaper in his mouth and ran back into the kitchen to give it to Mr Green. Amber ran after him and returned a few moments later, dragging part of the paper behind her.

"Hey, look at that!" laughed Sam. "She even wants to carry the paper!"

Tom laughed too.

Amber dropped the bit of newspaper she was carrying. Why were they laughing at her? "I'll practise," she miaowed. "Then you'll see – I can be just like a dog."

When Tom arrived to deliver the newspaper the next day, Amber was waiting on the mat. She had a piece of paper in her mouth.

Tom peeped through the letterbox and saw her. "Clever kitten!" he laughed. Amber purred. She liked being praised.

Soon after breakfast Mrs Green opened the back door and let all three dogs into the garden.

Amber was just about to sneak out with them when Mr Green stopped her. "No, Amber," he said. "You can't go out there yet." He shut the door firmly.

Amber sat on the mat and looked up at him. "Why not?" she miaowed.

But Mr Green had hurried away. He was late for work.

Amber jumped up onto the window sill to watch Jordan, Buster and Laddie chasing round the garden. "Are you having a good game?" she miaowed, but they didn't seem to hear her.

When Sam came downstairs for breakfast, he ran over to Amber and picked her up. He held her gently against his chest. "You can go out in the garden when you're older," he said, stroking the back of Amber's head. "When you've had your injections."

"Injections?" Amber miaowed.

"All cats have them when they're nine weeks old and twelve weeks old," Sam went on. "It's to stop you from getting ill. Your first one's today, at the vet's."

When Sam lifted Amber into the cardboard cat carrier that afternoon, Amber felt

frightened. She didn't know what to expect
when she got to the vet's.

But the vet had a kind face and a soft voice.
Amber soon forgot her fear. She was so busy
looking round the strange new place that she
hardly noticed the tiny prick on her neck.

"That wasn't so bad, was it?" the vet said,
smiling.

"Oh! Was that it?" miaowed Amber, as
Sam placed her back in the cat carrier.

★ ★ ★

Over the next few weeks, Amber learned to roll over and play dead, chase balls and carry bigger and bigger pieces of paper in her mouth. But she was dying to play out in the garden.

It seemed such a long time, waiting to be twelve weeks old!

At last, Amber had her second injection. And the next day, when the dogs were let out into the garden, Amber was allowed out, too. "Wait for me!" she miaowed, as they all tumbled out and raced off down the lawn. But the dogs weren't used to having Amber outside with them yet, and they forgot about her at first.

Amber stood by the step and looked around. Now she was in it, the garden seemed enormous! She stepped onto the grass. It was soft and rather wet.

She padded through it, slowly at first. Then she grew braver. She began to run. There was so much to explore!

Soon she was following Buster, Laddie and Jordan as they raced about.

It was the best fun she had ever had!

Later on, when Sam came home from school, he dashed into the garden to play with them. He threw sticks for them to chase. Amber did her best to reach the sticks first, but her tiny legs didn't carry her fast enough.

Sam saw what was happening. He called the dogs to heel, then threw a tiny stick, just for Amber.

Amber streaked after it, picked it up and brought it back to drop at Sam's feet.

"Well done!" he laughed.

"I'm getting more like a dog every day!" Amber miaowed proudly.

She raced off after the dogs, who had gone to see what Mr Green was doing. He had cut a hole in the back door and was fixing a flap over it.

"That's for you, Amber," he said, showing her how to use it with his hand.

"Try it."

Cautiously, Amber pushed her nose against the flap. It moved, so that she could walk through the hole, into the kitchen.

She turned round and came back out into the garden. "That's great!" she miaowed. "Now I can go in and out whenever I want!"

The following morning, Amber saw the dogs sitting by the front door. It was time for Sam to walk to school and, usually, Mrs Green and the dogs kept him company.

Amber got excited. Now that she'd been outside, perhaps she'd be allowed to go too. She went and sat beside them.

"Not you, Amber," Sam said. "Cats don't go for walks. Besides," he smiled, "we only have three leads!" He clipped them on to the dogs' collars.

After they had left, Amber walked miserably into the sitting-room and leapt onto an armchair. She'd have a snooze while they were out, she decided. The only good thing about being a cat was being allowed to sleep on the furniture! That was something the dogs weren't allowed to do!

But then Amber remembered her new cat

flap. *I could sneak out and follow them!* she thought excitedly.

Amber leapt out of the chair and ran into the kitchen. She pushed her way through the cat flap and sped down the back garden. She could hear Laddie yapping to the other two as usual, and followed the noise.

Climbing over the garden fence, Amber raced through an alley that led out on to Liberty Street. She was just in time to see Mrs Green, Sam and the dogs turning the corner.

Amber raced on after them. What an adventure! She had never gone further than the garden before. Her heart was racing with excitement, but she felt nervous, too. There were so many different sounds and smells.

Keeping close to the hedges and walls, Amber followed the dogs along Liberty Street and round the corner into a busier road. The noise of the traffic and the bustle of so many people almost made her turn back. *But if I want to be a dog, I'll have to act like one*, she thought. Buster, Jordan and Laddie are brave and so am I!

Mrs Green and Sam came to a part of the road that was striped. Amber watched them stop, then walk across the stripes to get to the other side. She was just about to follow when she heard her name.

"Amber? It is Amber, isn't it?"

Amber looked up at the lady who had spoken to her. It was Tom Bradman's gran, Mrs Jennings, wearing her big white coat. Mrs Jennings was a lollipop lady. She stopped the traffic with a big stick, so children on their way to school could cross the road.

"Yes," miaowed Amber. "Only I'm trying to be a dog."

"You shouldn't be out on your own," said Mrs Jennings. She looked across the road at Sam and Mrs Green.

"I'm trying to catch them up," miaowed Amber. "So I can go for a walk with them."

"Mrs Green!" called Mrs Jennings. "Sam!"

Mrs Green and Sam turned round and saw Amber. "Oh no!" Amber heard Sam shout worriedly. "Amber shouldn't be here, by the main road – it's dangerous!"

"I'll take her home if you like," called Mrs Jennings. "I finish here in a couple of minutes."

"Thanks," called Mrs Green. "I'd be very grateful. My husband's at home to answer the door."

But Amber wanted to do things by herself. So before Mrs Jennings could pick her up, she darted away, back along the busy road to Liberty Street.

A black kitten appeared from the shop on the corner. It was Jet, Amber's brother.

"Hello, Jet," Amber miaowed. "Do you live here, then?"

"Yes," miaowed Jet. "What have you been doing?"

"I was trying to be a dog and go for a walk," miaowed Amber. "But I didn't get very far. I'm on my way home."

A shadow-grey kitten padded down from some steps nearby and came to join in the conversation. It was their sister, Emerald, who also lived in Liberty Street.

"Hello, Emerald," miaowed Amber. She was really pleased to see her brother and sister. But before they could talk any more, Amber saw Mrs Jennings coming along to look for her. Not wanting to get into more trouble, she ran off home.

3

A few minutes later, Amber sat in Laddie's box feeling very sorry for herself. After speaking with Mrs Jennings, Mr Green had firmly locked the cat flap.

"I hate being a cat!" Amber mewed. "Why can't I be a dog?" She thought about Jet and Emerald. They seemed to like being cats. Amber couldn't imagine why.

The cat flap stayed locked the next time

her friends went out for a walk. And the next time. In fact the Greens seemed determined to stop her going with them. Amber felt really fed up. *Will I ever be able to go for a walk, like a dog?* she wondered.

Her chance came sooner than she expected. One Saturday afternoon, the Greens forgot to lock the cat-flap. Amber waited for them to leave, then she ran straight through the cat-flap, over the garden fence and down the alley into Liberty Street.

The Greens weren't walking towards Sam's school this time – they were going the other way. Amber followed them, staying hidden by jumping from garden to garden down the street.

Soon they came to the edge of town. All Amber could see ahead was open green space. *Wow!* she thought.

Sam let the dogs off their leads and they bounded off. This open countryside was a new experience for Amber and her heart beat fast. She wanted to stop and sniff at everything and explore this new place. But more than that, she wanted to play in all this space with Buster, Jordan and Laddie.

Suddenly she heard Laddie bark and he came running towards her, followed by Buster and Jordan. The three dogs ran rings round Amber, barking loudly.

"Shh!" miaowed Amber. "Don't let them know I'm here."

But it was too late. Sam came running over. "What have you found?" he called to the dogs. "A rabbit?"

He stopped and stared. "Oh, no!" he cried. "Mum, Dad! Who forgot to lock the cat flap?"

"We'll have to go back," said Mrs Green when she saw the naughty kitten.

Mr Green nodded. "We can't have her following us any further."

"Why not?" miaowed Amber. "I'm not any trouble."

"Why not?" asked Sam. "She does everything else that dogs do, so why can't she come for a walk?"

"Thanks, Sam!" miaowed Amber. "That's

what I've been waiting to hear!"

Mrs Green laughed. "Oh, all right," she said. "If that cat's so determined to be a dog!"

Amber was glad she didn't have to stay hidden any more. It was wonderful to race through the fields with her three friends. But when they came to a farmyard Sam picked her up. "We have to walk more slowly through here," he said. "So we don't frighten the animals."

Mr and Mrs Green kept Buster, Jordan and Laddie on their leads until they came to open fields again. Then Sam put Amber down to run with the dogs again.

All of sudden, Amber heard a snort. What's that? She turned to look and froze with surprise. An enormous brown animal was staring fiercely at them all. It had wild brown eyes, a big ring through its nose and two very sharp-looking horns!

Mrs Green screamed

"A bull! shouted Mr Green. "Run!"

"What's a bull?" Amber miaowed. But everyone had started running. Mr Green led the way across the field, pulling Mrs Green by the hand. Mrs Green had grabbed Sam and was dragging him along behind her. The dogs bounded speedily ahead of them towards the gate at the side of the field.

"Come on, Amber," Sam shouted over his shoulder.

But the bull had rounded on Amber and stood in her way. "You don't seem very friendly," she miaowed nervously.

"I'm not!" roared the bull.

Amber began to tremble. "Help!" she mewed. Then, out of the corner of her eye, she noticed a tree near by. *I can climb that!* she thought. The bull took his eyes off her to watch the others, as they climbed the fence to safety. Amber took her chance. She streaked away from him and began to haul herself up the tree, faster than she'd ever climbed before. *Quick, quick*, she said to herself, as she dug her claws into the bark.

Amber was halfway up the trunk when the bull turned back and saw she was gone. With a roar that echoed through the branches, he

lost interest and lumbered off to the other end of the field.

Thank goodness I'm a cat! Amber thought for the first time ever. *Dogs can't climb trees!*

Checking that the bull wasn't looking, Amber jumped down from the tree. Then making herself as low as possible to the ground, she scuttled across the field to the fence, to join the others. "Hello!" she miaowed.

"Amber!" Sam cried. "You're safe!"

"I thought the bull must have got you!" barked Jordan.

"It's a good job cats can climb trees!" said Mrs Green. "That must have saved your life, Amber!"

"I know!" miaowed Amber.

"Come on," said Mr Green. "Let's go home."

They had almost reached their house in Liberty Street when a black kitten jumped down from a wall in front of them. Amber heard Mrs Green gasp.

"Oh! It made me jump!" she said. "My nerves are shattered by that bull!"

But Amber knew who it was. "Hello, Jet," she miaowed. "We've just had a great adventure."

"So you managed to go on your walk!" miaowed Jet.

The kittens touched noses and Amber told Jet about the bull and how she had climbed the tree to escape from it.

"Well done," purred Jet. "Now perhaps you'll agree that being a cat is best!"

"Mmm," Amber miaowed. "Maybe you're right!"

Jet

1

Jet sat in the doorway of the corner shop in the warm sunshine. It was the best place to be if you wanted to see everything that was going on. And Jet did!

Mrs Jennings was walking towards him along the pavement. Jet was used to watching Mrs Jennings out on the busy road, helping children to cross over on their way to school. She would walk into the striped part of the road, hold her stick up and stop the cars.

Mrs Jennings always walked past the corner shop at the same time, on her way home. "Hello, Jet!" she said when she reached him. "Looking after the shop, as usual?"

Jet stood up and rubbed the side of his face against Mrs Jennings' legs. "Of course I am," he miaowed. "They always need my help."

"You're such a handsome boy," said Mrs Jennings as she bent to stroke his gleaming black coat. Then she chuckled. "Black cats are two a penny," she said, "but you're the only one I've ever met with a pure white tip to your tail!"

"Thank you," purred Jet. He was proud of that white tip. Lots of people admired it.

"I've just got to pop into the shop for a loaf of bread," said Mrs Jennings. "Coming?"

Jet followed Mrs Jennings through the open doorway and into the shop. He jumped up onto the counter by a pile of fresh bread. But immediately, two strong hands lifted him down again.

Jet looked up to see who had put him back

on the floor. It was Steve. He and Angie, his wife, ran the corner shop. Jet had come to live with them when he'd left the Bradmans' house as a tiny kitten.

"I don't mind you up with the tins and packets, Jet," Steve said firmly, "but you know you shouldn't be near the fresh food."

"Sorry!" Jet miaowed. Steve had told him several times, but he kept forgetting. "I was only trying to help." He rubbed against Steve's ankles. "Are we still friends?"

Steve smiled down at Jet, then grinned at Mrs Jennings. He was always smiling and friendly. Jet loved him.

Mrs Jennings smiled back. "It seems like only yesterday that Jet was one of Bracken's newborn kittens," she said. Jet's mum, Bracken, lived nearby in Liberty Street with Mrs Jennings's daughter and her family.

Just then, Angie came through into the shop from the room at the back. "I know, she said, "but Jet's almost a year old now! I remember Tom was so excited when he came into the shop to collect the papers on the morning Bracken's kittens were born. It made us want to have one." Tom was Mrs Jenning's grandson and he delivered newspapers for Angie and Steve.

Jet listened to Angie talking. He loved her high, sing-song voice.

When Angie and Steve had brought Jet to his new home all those months ago, he'd had a wonderful surprise. He remembered the first time he had explored the shelves and cupboards, with their exciting smells. And he still found new corners to explore and boxes to sniff.

Then, when Jet was twelve weeks old, Steve had put a cat-flap in the side entrance to the shop, where the deliveries were made. It meant that Jet could come and go as he pleased. It was a brilliant place to live!

Mrs Jennings paid for her loaf of bread. "Oh, I forgot to ask," she said to Angie as she headed for the door. "How are you?"

"Very well, thanks," said Angie. "But I

seem to be getting bigger every day!" she laughed.

She has become rather plump lately! Jet thought to himself.

The next morning, when Tom Bradman collected his newspapers to deliver, Jet helped him load his bag.

"Get out of the bag, Jet!" Tom laughed.

"But you like me helping you," Jet miaowed.

Tom picked him up for a moment and gave him a cuddle.

"I remember you coming to collect the papers on the first morning I was here," Jet purred. "I was afraid you'd come to take me away from Angie and Steve. But once I knew I could stay in my nice new home, I was really happy to see you."

Tom put Jet down and picked up his heavy bag. "See you tomorrow," he said as he left the shop.

"I look forward to it!" Jet miaowed. But before he saw Tom again, he had the rest of the day to enjoy. He couldn't wait to meet today's customers. They would pet him and admire his silky black coat and comment on his unusual white-tipped tail. It was great being the star attraction!

"Oh no!"

Just then, Jet heard Angie's voice, much higher and louder than usual, coming from the storeroom behind the shop. He padded over to see what was the matter.

"What's up?" asked Steve who had hurried downstairs from their flat above the shop.

"Look!" cried Angie, pointing at a corner behind some boxes. "Mouse droppings!"

Steve and Jet went to investigate. Jet sniffed around the corner and his whiskers twitched with excitement. *Ooh, where's that mouse? I'd love it for my dinner!* he thought.

"It's even nibbled the cheese, without getting caught!" said Angie. Steve had put down a trap to try and catch the mouse.

Steve sighed. "I'd better try again," he said as Angie sat down on a set of steps. "We'll be in trouble from the health inspectors if we have mice in the shop."

Angie looked hot and bothered and Jet hated to see her upset.

"Sorry!" said Steve, bending to kiss her. "I'll set it again tonight."

"And I'll see what I can do," miaowed Jet.

"You go and have a rest, Angie," said Steve gently. "I'll manage the shop this morning."

"Thanks, I get so tired at the moment," she said with a smile. "Call me if you need me."

Jet watched Angie heave herself up from the steps and waddle to the stairs. She really had got bigger lately!

When she had gone upstairs, Steve went into the shop. Jet stayed behind to prowl about, looking for the mouse. The scent of mouse was very strong. But there was no sign of it.

Just then, Jet heard Mrs Jennings' voice in the shop. She must be on her way to work at the zebra crossing. "I'll catch you later, mouse," Jet hissed, then he ran into the shop to greet his friend.

★ ★ ★

Very early the next morning, Jet trotted upstairs before Angie and Steve were up. Their bedroom door was shut so he sat outside and called. "Wake up," he yowled. "Open the door. I've got a surprise for you."

"Whatever's wrong with Jet?" he heard Angie say.

"I've got something to show you!" miaowed Jet, lifting his paw to scratch at the door.

The door opened. Steve stood there, half-dressed, blinking in the darkness of the landing. "What is it, Jet?" he asked.

"You wanted that mouse caught," said Jet. "So here it is!"

"Hey, Angie!" Steve called. "He's caught the mouse. Well done, you clever cat!"

He lifted Jet with the mouse still in his mouth for Angie to see. "Brilliant!" said Angie, who was sitting up in bed. "You're better than any mousetrap, Jet. I name you 'Chief Mouser'!"

"Thanks!" miaowed Jet proudly. "I like that!"

Grinning, Steve took the mouse from Jet and carried it downstairs. "I'll put it outside the side door for you," he said.

Half an hour later, when Tom came to collect the newspapers for his round, Jet was walking about the shop with his head and tail held high.

"You look pleased with yourself," said Tom. "What have you been up to?"

"I'm Chief Mouser!" miaowed Jet.

"He caught a mouse during the night," said Steve. "He's Chief Mouser from now on."

Jet couldn't wait for it to get dark so that he could try to catch another mouse. He had smelled mice before, behind the shop and under the steps that led up to the flats next door. His sister, Emerald, lived in one of the flats with George. Perhaps she can be my Assistant Mouser! Jet thought.

Emerald came by the corner shop later that day to say hello to Jet.

"What do you think?" miaowed Jet after he had told his sister his plan.

"I'd love to be Assistant Mouser," Emerald replied. "I could do with some practice."

So, that night, Jet and Emerald prowled the area. When Jet brought home his share of the catch Angie and Steve were delighted.

"Well done!" Angie said when Jet presented them with the mice.

Later that afternoon, Mrs Bradman, Tom's mum, came into the shop on her way home from work. "It's lovely to see all our kittens growing up into such handsome cats," she said, picking Jet up and stroking him.

"Not just handsome . . ." said Angie.

". . . like his owner . . ." added Steve.

". . . but clever, too . . .!" said Angie, grinning at her husband.

". . . unlike his owner!" finished Steve roaring with laughter.

Laughing too, Angie explained. "What Steve means," she said, "is that Jet is better at catching mice than he is!"

"Well done, Jet!" said Mrs Bradman, tickling the sides of Jet's face. "Our Bracken will be so proud when I tell her."

2

The next day, a boy and his mum came into the shop. His mum also had a baby in a buggy. Jet decided to hide behind a box. The boy looked all right, but Jet wasn't sure if he liked babies. This one was making lots of strange gurgling noises!

"Hello, Sue. How are you?" said Angie, leaning over the counter to look at the baby. "And how's little Hannah?"

"We're really well, thanks," said Sue. "And how about you?"

"Fine," smiled Angie. "Apart from looking like a balloon!"

"How much longer now?" asked Sue.

"Just a couple of weeks," said Angie.

While his mum and Angie were talking, the boy explored the shop and noticed Jet behind his box. "Hello, puss!" he said, bending to stroke the kitten. "Are you hiding?"

Jet began to purr, enjoying the fuss. "Not from you," he miaowed. "I like you! But I'm not quite sure about your baby sister, yet. She seems a bit frightening!"

"Da da da da da," Hannah said loudly. Jet crouched lower behind the box.

"Colin!" the boy's mum called. "Come and help choose a birthday card for Dad."

Colin hurried over to the counter where the shelf of greetings cards were displayed.

Jet followed, creeping nearer to Hannah, who was bashing a toy against the buggy with a big smile on her face.

"Where's Steve this morning?" Sue asked Angie.

"Out the back, sorting out a delivery that's just come in," said Angie.

Sue nodded. "Now, what do I want?" she said. "Let me see. A sliced loaf, a tin of baked beans and some eggs."

"Ga ga ga, ga ga GAAA!" said Hannah even louder.

Jet dashed back behind his box, deciding babies were very scary. He watched in surprise, as Angie smiled and wiggled her finger at Hannah while Sue fetched the groceries she needed. Angie seemed to like babies.

Then Hannah began to make soft gurgling sounds instead. Jet didn't mind those so much, so he decided to take another look. He poked his head out from behind the box, watching Hannah carefully, in case she started to make frightening noises again.

Hannah noticed him and pointed her finger. "Goo goo, gurgle gurgle," she went softly.

Jet began to feel less afraid. He crawled forward a little. Perhaps she wants to be friends, he thought.

"I think Hannah likes you, Jet," said Angie from behind the counter.

Sue came back with a basket full of food and Angie began ringing it into the till.

"Da da da da da da da," said Hannah, waving her arms above her head.

The baby's noise was getting a bit loud again, so Jet hung back a little, still watching. Then he crept forward, curious to see more. "You're a strange creature," he miaowed.

"Ga ga ga ga ga ga," Hannah burbled. Then she put her fingers in her mouth and began to chew them.

Angie and Sue were busy chatting and laughing. And Colin was still looking at the birthday cards for dads.

Jet stalked around Hannah's buggy, looking at her. She chuckled, kicking her legs and clapping her hands. He sniffed the air. She had a different kind of scent, a sweet smell that reminded Jet of when Angie had a bath.

"Da da da da da da," said Hannah again, pointing her chubby finger and waving her arms.

Slowly, Jet grew used to the baby's movements and noises. She didn't seem to want to hurt him. Perhaps he could get near enough for her to stroke him. Then they could be friends.

He pushed his nose against the buggy, then rubbed the side of his face along it, letting Hannah touch him.

Hannah squealed loudly with delight. Frightened, Jet backed away. But then she became quiet again, so he couldn't resist creeping closer again.

The baby reached out her arms and ruffled Jet's fur with her tiny hands. It felt quite nice! "You're not as scary as I thought," Jet miaowed.

"Goo goo goo goo," Hannah cooed as she poked Jet's ears then touched his long white whiskers.

He began to walk round and round the buggy. Hannah swivelled round as Jet went by and stretched out to touch him, giggling. I'm beginning to like this strange little person! Jet thought.

Then suddenly, Hannah lunged towards him. Her tiny hand grasped the white tip of his tail. Jet felt the grip tighten. "Da da da da da da!" she shouted as she pulled Jet's tail as hard as she could!

"Owww!" yowled Jet as a sharp pain shot

up his back. "Let go!" he hissed. "Let go! Yowww!"

As suddenly as she had grabbed the tail, Hannah let go. She threw herself against the back of her buggy, opened her mouth very wide and screamed. "Wa wa wa wa wa wa!"

Frightened out of his wits, Jet leapt up onto the counter, his back arched and his fur standing on end. "How dare you pull my tail!" he hissed down at the baby. "It really hurt!"

Sue and Angie stopped talking and Colin dropped the pile of cards he was holding.

"Jet!" Angie cried, shocked.

Sue lifted Hannah out of the buggy and began rocking her. "Your cat attacked Hannah!" she shouted at Angie. Hannah's screaming grew louder.

Angie looked at Jet as if she couldn't believe it. "But Jet's such a good-natured cat," she said.

"Yes, Mum," Colin agreed. "I was stroking that kitten earlier – he's really gentle."

"Well, he'd better not have scratched her!" shouted Sue. "There there," she said in a high little voice as she inspected Hannah. "Did that nasty cat go for you?"

"Wa wa wa wa wa wa," went the baby.

Sue turned on Angie. "You need to control that cat!" she said.

"I've never seen Jet hiss like that before," Angie argued back. "Hannah must have frightened him!"

Jet looked down at the angry women. *They're both very cross and it's all my fault. Maybe I shouldn't have hissed like that.* He turned his head to inspect the tip of his tail. *But she really hurt me!*

Just then the door opened at the back of the shop and Steve rushed in.

"What's going on?" he asked.

"Your cat attacked Hannah," Sue said.

"He didn't!" shouted Angie, whose face had gone rather red. "Hannah frightened him!"

"Calm down, love," Steve said, putting his arm round Angie. "It's not good for you to get so worked up."

"Hannah was only playing!" shouted Sue.

"But Mum!" Colin said, bending down to pick up the cards he'd dropped. "You know how hard Hannah sometimes pulls our hair when she's playing. Perhaps she did the same thing to the kitten."

"Yes, yes!" mewed Jet from his hiding-place on the counter. "You're right!"

"That's different!" shouted Colin's mum. Then Hannah starting crying so loudly that no one could hear themselves speak.

"Now, now," said Steve hurriedly. "I suggest that we forget all this, then Sue can pay for her groceries and go home."

"Pay for my groceries?" Sue said, crossly. "I'm not buying anything from here, thank you!"

She put the still-screaming Hannah back in the buggy and stormed from the shop, calling, "Come on, Colin – we're late!"

As soon as the baby had gone, Jet jumped down from the counter. Colin gave a sheepish smile to Angie and Steve, then patted Jet and followed his mum.

"Thanks for sticking up for me!" Jet purred after him. Then he ran round the counter to Angie and Steve. "I didn't mean to upset that baby," he miaowed, "but she hurt me."

Angie and Steve didn't seem to hear him, so he rubbed the side of his face against Angie's legs, but instead of stroking him as usual, she began to cry. "Sue didn't have to be so nasty," she said.

"It's OK, she was just worried about Hannah," Steve said, hugging her. "Now you must calm down."

Jet twined himself around Angie's legs but she was too busy wiping her eyes to notice him. "Come on, let's put these groceries back where they belong," she said, taking a deep breath.

Normally, Angie and Steve would have let Jet help them, but their usual cheery faces looked sad and they were only interested in putting everything away. They seemed to have forgotten all about him. He watched them return the unwanted food to the shelves, then crept silently out of the door into the street.

They've lost a customer because of me. No wonder they were cross! Jet thought.

Emerald was sitting in a corner at the bottom of the steps that led up to the flats. Jet didn't see her at first because she was hidden in the shadows. But when she turned to talk to him he saw her emerald eyes glinting. "Hello," she miaowed. "You look rather miserable."

"I am," miaowed Jet sadly. "Angie and Steve are cross with me. They don't want to talk to me any more."

"Why? What have you done?" miaowed Emerald.

When Jet had told her about Hannah, Emerald stood up and walked over to him. She rubbed her nose against his. "I'm sure they're not really cross with you," she miaowed. "It's not like them to be cross with anyone!"

"I know," miaowed Jet. "That's why I'm so unhappy. They've always been so kind to me. The last thing I want to do is upset them."

Just then the front door at the top of the steps opened. The two kittens looked up. "Emerald, supper time!" It was George, Emerald's owner.

"I've got to go," said Emerald, scampering up the steps. "Don't worry!"

"I'll try not to," mewed Jet to himself after his sister had gone indoors. "But what if Angie and Steve never forgive me?"

He curled up sadly and put his head on his paws. He just couldn't bear the thought of it.

3

Jet didn't go home until evening. He thought it was best to stay out of Angie and Steve's way. But when the sun started to go down, he felt hungry.

He went to the side entrance and pushed the cat flap with his nose. There was no sign of Angie or Steve, but a dish of cat food had been left there for him. He jumped inside and began to eat hungrily. *Perhaps they're not too cross with me*, he thought to himself.

When he had finished the food, Jet crept over to the stairs that led up to the flat. The sitting-room door was open a crack and he could see the light was on. Angie and Steve must be in there, he thought.

"I'm so uncomfortable." Angie's voice floated down the stairs. She didn't sound cross any more! But she didn't sound her usual happy self, either. Jet thought he would leave them alone for a while longer. The mice would be coming out now it was getting dark. He would go and see if he could catch any.

Jet spent a long time sniffing around the front of the shop. There didn't seem to be any mice about. He began to feel sleepy and so went inside to look for somewhere to curl up. He found an empty cardboard box and jumped in. Usually he curled up in his basket in the kitchen but he decided to leave it until the morning to go upstairs. Surely Angie and Steve would have forgiven him by the morning.

He didn't feel like he'd been asleep for long when he heard Tom arriving to collect his newspapers. Jet peeked into the shop. Steve was rushing around, sorting the papers and filling the delivery bags. Usually, Jet would have jumped up to help Steve, but he thought he would let him do it on his own today.

"Hello, Jet," said Tom, noticing him. "You're quiet this morning."

"Steve's not very pleased with me," miaowed Jet.

Just then, Angie called from upstairs. "Steve! Come quickly!" Her voice was shrill.

What's the matter with Angie? Jet thought. *What could be so urgent?*

"I'm coming," Steve shouted. He hurriedly handed Tom his full bag, and then ran up the stairs two at a time without stopping to talk to Jet.

"Good luck," shouted Tom, as he left the shop.

Everything's different this morning! Jet couldn't believe everyone had left him in the shop on his own. Then he had another surprise. Steve came bounding back down the stairs, carrying a suitcase.

Jet couldn't understand it. The last time Jet had seen Steve carrying a case like that he and Angie had gone away for a week. But they told me about it first, Jet thought. And they left someone to look after the shop and feed me!

"I'll get the car out," Steve called up the stairs and then dashed out of the shop.

"All right," Angie called back. Her voice sounded very strange! She was coming down the stairs very slowly. She had a deep frown on her face and she kept stopping to hold onto the banisters.

"What's wrong?" miaowed Jet.

"Not now, Jet," Angie said, not even looking at him. She held her hand under her big tummy as she walked past him and out of the door. Then she switched out the lights and turned the key in the lock!

Jet heard the *vroom vroom* of the car engine starting, then doors slamming and the car driving away. He just couldn't understand it. He sat still for a while and then washed himself while he had a think. He would go outside and see if there were any clues.

He jumped out through the cat flap and went round to the front of the shop on Liberty Street. But nothing looked any different. Jet just couldn't understand it.

He watched people come up to the shop then walk away shaking their heads when they found it closed. "I don't know what's going on either!" Jet miaowed after them

While Jet was stretched out in a front garden halfway along the street, a golden tabby came up to him. It was his sister, Amber.

"Emerald tells me you're in trouble with your owners," she miaowed.

"Yes, and now they've gone away," miaowed Jet.

"Gone away?" miaowed Amber, sitting down beside him. "Where to?"

When Jet had told Amber the whole story, she nuzzled gently against his face. "Emerald also told me Angie named you her Chief Mouser," she miaowed. "Why don't you see if you can catch some mice to show them when they come home? They'd like that, wouldn't they?"

"Good idea. Will you help me?" Jet miaowed, feeling a bit more cheerful. But secretly he was worried that Angie and Steve weren't coming home. What if they hadn't forgiven him for upsetting the baby?

It was dark when Jet heard the familiar sound of Steve's car coming along the road. He sat waiting inside the shop with several mice that he and Amber had caught together. A key turned in the lock and Steve pushed open the door and switched on the light. But where was Angie?

"I've brought you some presents," Jet miaowed.

Steve bent and stroked his head. "Good boy," he said with a smile. Jet was so glad to see that smile! Steve didn't seem upset any more, but he didn't pick him up or make more of a fuss of him. He just put the dead mice outside the side door, then ran upstairs. Jet could hear him singing. *But why does he sound so happy if Angie isn't here?* he wondered.

The shop door opened and two men came in. "Steve!" they called. Jet heard Steve's feet thundering down the stairs.

"Hello!" Steve said as he ran into the shop.

"We just heard the news," said one of the men. "Well done!"

What news?

"Congratulations!" said the other man. He patted Steve on the back and Steve laughed.

Jet looked from one to the other. *What's going on? Why are they congratulating Steve?* He felt very confused.

All through the next day, lots more people came into the shop, laughing and joking and thumping Steve on the back. But no one seemed to notice Jet. *It's almost as if I've become invisible!* he thought, sadly. *I wish Angie would come back.*

The only person to pay him any attention all day was the boy, Colin. He walked past the shop with his dad when Jet was sitting on the pavement washing his paws.

"I know you didn't hurt my baby sister," he said, bending down to stroke Jet.

"Thanks," Jet purred loudly, as Colin ran off to catch up with his dad.

That evening, when Steve closed the shop he drove away in the car again. But this time Jet didn't have to wait so long for him to return. He was sitting on the path outside the shop doorway when the car stopped next to the kerb. And there, sitting in the back of the car, was Angie!

Steve opened the car door and Angie climbed out. Her fat tummy had gone and she was carrying a white bundle in her arms. *What's in there?* Jet wondered.

Steve opened the shop door and they went inside and up the stairs to their flat. Jet followed. He wanted to know what they had brought home.

When they reached the sitting-room, Angie sat down on the sofa and unwrapped the white bundle. Jet stood staring in amazement. It was pink and small with a wrinkled face . . . it was a baby! He couldn't believe that Angie and Steve had brought a baby home.

Jet flattened his ears and scuttled to the safety of the sideboard. There was just enough room for him to squeeze underneath it. He pressed his nose against the wall at the back of the sideboard, hoping that Angie and Steve wouldn't notice him.

But he'd forgotten to tuck in his tail!

"Come out of there, Jet, you silly thing!" said Steve. "I can see the white tip of your tail." He spoke in such a friendly voice that Jet backed out from his hiding-place.

Steve picked Jet up and held him against his chest. Jet nuzzled against him and smelled his familiar scent. He was beginning to feel better now that Steve was behaving more like his old self.

"Jet, this is the new member of our family," Steve said. "She's a little girl."

"I hope Jet gets on with her," said Angie anxiously.

Jet looked over at the tiny baby in her arms, his whiskers twitching. "I'll like anything if it means you won't disappear again," he miaowed. "But I'd prefer it if she doesn't pull my tail!"

As Steve carried him closer to the sofa, Jet dug his claws into his sweater. He still wasn't sure if he wanted to go near the baby. Steve sat down next to Angie and gently unhooked Jet's claws. "Calm down, boy," he said with a big smile. "Don't worry. This baby's not going to hurt you."

Jet began to feel happy again. Angie and Steve still wanted him after all.

Angie reached over to stroke him. "Poor old Jet," she said. "First you have the fright of your life when your tail is pulled. Then we're too busy getting me off to the hospital to notice you. No wonder you're not sure what to make of it all."

"I have been a bit worried. But everything's OK now you're home again," Jet purred. He looked at the baby lying asleep in Angie's arms. Then he gingerly stepped off Steve's lap onto the sofa. Slowly, he crept towards the baby. She certainly looked harmless.

Suddenly, the baby stirred, opened her eyes and let out a cry. In split second, Jet had shot off the sofa and was sliding under the sideboard. But Angie's soft voice stopped him in his tracks.

"Jet," she called. "Come back. Don't be frightened. Just because the baby cries doesn't mean she's going to hurt you."

Jet turned around and looked at Angie. The

baby was still crying. Jet wasn't sure. But then Angie lifted her up to her shoulder. And as if by magic the crying stopped.

"Come on Jet – surely you're not scared? You're the brave Chief Mouser of the house," said Steve patting his lap for the kitten to climb on.

He's right, thought Jet. *I'm not scared of mice, so why should I be afraid of a baby?* So he jumped onto Steve's lap, then stepped next to Angie and peered at the baby. She had her eyes closed and was breathing noisily. Jet noticed that she smelled just like Angie. That was nice! Nice and comforting.

Jet nuzzled into Angie's arm, purring. "I think I could get to like your baby," he miaowed to Angie and Steve, flicking his white-tipped tail. "And perhaps I can teach her to leave my tail alone!"

**Nine Lives Book 1:
GINGER, NUTMEG AND CLOVE**

Bracken, the Bradmans' cat, has given birth to nine adorable kittens. Nine very different personalities each need very special homes. Can the Bradmans be sure they've found the right owners?

Red-haired *Ginger* is fearless and nosy – will he settle in with Amy and her mother? Or will he be too much of a handful?

Long-haired *Nutmeg* is really naughty and her new owners don't know how to keep her out of trouble. Until one day Nutmeg's inquisitiveness teaches her a lesson . . .

Clove doesn't seem too happy in her new home – and she won't eat the food that Mr Miller is giving her. Then the most unexpected person comes up with a solution . . .

Nine Lives Book 3:
DAISY, BUTTERCUP AND WEED

Bracken, the Bradmans' cat, has given birth to nine adorable kittens. Nine very different personalities each need very special homes. Can the Bradmans be sure they've found the right owners?

Snow-white *Daisy* is adorable – but very very quiet. What will make Daisy miaow for the first time?

Everyone wants to play with *Buttercup*. But can she please everybody at once?

Scrawny little *Weed* is the runt of the litter – who will want her? The Bradmans despair, but is the answer closer than they think?

The Nine Lives Trilogy by

LUCY DANIELS

0 340 73619 4	GINGER, NUGMEG AND CLOVE	£3.50 ❏
0 340 73621 6	DAISY, BUTTERCUP AND WEED	£3.50 ❏

All Hodder Children's books are available at your local bookshop or newsagent, or can be ordered direct from the publisher. Just tick the titles you want and fill in the form below. Prices and availability subject to change without notice.

Hodder Children's Books, Cash Sales Department, Bookpoint, 39 Milton Park, Abingdon, OXON, OX14 4TD, UK. If you have a credit card you may order by telephone, our call team would be delighted to take your order by telephone. Our direct line is *01235 400414* (lines open 9.00 am–6.00 pm Monday to Saturday, 24 hour message answering service). Alternatively you can send a fax on *01235 400454.*

Or please enclose a cheque or postal order made payable to Bookpoint Ltd to the value of the cover price and allow the following for postage and packing: UK & BFPO – £1.00 for the first book, 50p for the second book, and 30p for each additional book ordered up to a maximum charge of £3.00. OVERSEAS & EIRE – £2.00 for the first book, £1.00 for the second book, and 50p for each additional book.

Name ....

Address ....

....

....

If you would prefer to pay by credit card, please complete:
Please debit my Visa/Access/Diner's Card/American Express (delete as applicable) card no:

Signature ....

Expiry Date ....